The Boxcar
at the Center
of the
Universe

The Boxcar at the Center of the Universe

BY RICHARD KENNEDY

Illustrations by Jeff Kronen

Harper & Row, Publishers

4

Edward I

&

Edward II

The Boxcar at the Center of the Universe
Text copyright © 1982 by Richard Kennedy
Illustrations copyright © 1982 by Jeff Kronen
Printed in the United States of America. All rights
reserved.

Library of Congress Cataloging in Publication Data
Kennedy, Richard, 1932–
    The boxcar at the center of the universe.

    Summary: A sixteen-year-old boy on a journey of
discovery meets up with a tramp who tells him of his
own search for the center of the universe.
    [1. Arabs—Fiction.   2. Fantasy]   I. Kronen, Jeff,
ill.   II. Title.
PZ7.K385Bo 1982   [Fic]   81-47718
ISBN 0-06-023186-6   AACR2
ISBN 0-06-023187-4 (lib. bdg.)

First Edition

Contents

The Boxcar
at the Center
of the
Universe

The Beginning of Summer

The beginning of the summer of my sixteenth year was like a fresh idea, like a brand-new thought, like a cheering and praising of the weeks to come all awaiting my arrival. The planets wheeled for me alone, the sun and moon rose and set for me alone, the winds and rains clapped approval and the dawn leaped up like a clean rainbow fish out of the great clear lake of my expectation, and the days passed like crystal mirrors reflecting the joy in my heart and the singing in my soul that I was loved by the very light of the day.

I set off as bright and ready for use as new silver, as rich in wonder as Montezuma's gold, the awe of life rising in me like the pillared uprising of Atlantis to acclaim and anoint the common day a miracle. I was sixteen. I was as hopeful as first solutions and elemental discoveries. Sixteen! Lord of the Universe,

Champion of the Day and Rescuer of the Night. Columbus, Magellan, Cyrano on the way to the moon with nine dollars in my pocket, circumnavigating the universe by way up the Columbia River out of Portland to discover the Ten Thousand Things of the World, to explore the Nine-gated City of the Self, the Twelve Houses of the Heavens, the Seven Deadly Sins, the Three Fates, the One God, the Four Horsemen, the Nine Muses, and the Eight Beatitudes. What a proud and brave army I was. What an expedition! There had been no such going forth since the going forth of Ulysses, Alexander, Constantine, Caesar, Hannibal. . . . In eight weeks or so, I figured, I would have the world surrounded, a sure chart to all hidden places, and I would have made all the appointments for the future and correct governing of the earth.

So it began. Two days later I was lost, riding in a boxcar out of Pendleton with no money in my pocket and a suspicion that I had lice.

There was no work in Pendleton and the train was going elsewhere. Just where, I didn't know, so when I climbed aboard I was lost. I walked past the engine down the line of cars until I found an open boxcar. Looking both ways up and down the track and seeing no one, I pushed my backpack inside, hauled myself through the door, and crawled over scattered straw and rough boards heavily bolted. Even before reaching the other side of the car, I heard the whoop of a yell outside and the sound of the yanked couplings coming down the line. Then my boxcar jolted and we were off and rolling, smooth and heavy. In the distance I could hear the struggling engine. Crawling to the far side of the car, I leaned my back up against the closed door on that side. Then I undid my belt and scratched at my stomach. A voice came from the other side of the boxcar.

An Old Bum and Goats in the Sky

"Been riding with sheep?"

'Huh?" I said. Someone was sitting next to the bright rectangle of the open door across from me. My eyes weren't used to the dimness and I couldn't make him out. It was an old man's voice.

"You don't want to ride with sheep," he said. "They can give you a bad influence. Ticks, you understand. I wouldn't ride with sheep. Cattle are all right, if you don't get stepped on. Goats if you want, but I wouldn't ride with sheep."

"I don't think it's ticks," I said, still scratching.

"Where'd you sleep last night?"

"In a . . . sort of place," I said. I wasn't ready to use the word "flophouse" yet.

"Maybe lice," the voice said.

That's what I thought, too, and now I could see my companion. Just an old bum, dressed in old bummy clothes and wearing a bummy hat. Next to him was an old bummy packsack. There were his sort in the flophouse I had stayed in, forgotten and wandering old men, lying on lumpy mattresses, all with the same voice. Half the night, scratching at myself, I listened to their snoring, coughing, and midnight

callings in their dreams to people and places lost long ago.

"You like goats?" the old bum asked.

"I don't know," I said, buckling my belt again. "I suppose they're all right."

"They ain't bad animals," he said. "No future in them, but they're all right. Smart. Friendly, too, almost like pets. We used to raise goats, when I was young."

I nodded and scratched at a leg. We were silent, and I looked out the great rectangle of the sliding door at the golden day. A few houses went past, horses grazed, children played. We seemed to be heading north, going alongside a slow stream. I saw a boy fishing on the opposite bank. He looked up from his reflection in the water and waved at the train.

"Once I saw some goats walking upside down in the sky," the old bum said.

I kept looking out the door for a few moments, then I looked at him. "Is that so?" I said it politely enough. After all, he was in the boxcar before I was, and my host in a way. The light from the door moved across his face as we rounded a curve. He looked even older than his voice sounded. He had a long white beard. Too early to know if he was crazy. He combed through his beard with his fingers, staring back at me, making his own study. It made me uncomfortable, so I spoke.

"Goats walking upside down in the sky," I said. "You wouldn't see that every day, I guess."

"That's how it looked, anyway," he said. "See, I was in a pitch-dark tent, sick with a fever, and all of a sudden I saw a picture on the tent wall of goats walking upside down in the sky. At first I thought I was dreaming, but I wasn't. Just a little trick of nature, that's all it was. But those upside-down goats sure got me into a lot of trouble."

"Uh-huh," I grunted, digging down the back of my pants for a scratch.

Lost in the Desert and Something About a King

"Just about your age," the old bum said, "when I saw those goats walking upside down in the sky. Strange sight. That's how it all began, and it ended with me being lost in the desert with five friends, dying of thirst."

"Eastern Oregon?" I said.

"Oh, hell no—Sahara Desert. Born and raised in the Sahara Desert. I'm an Arab, you know."

He didn't look like an Arab, and he didn't talk like an Arab, either. Looked and talked like an old bum. He saw that I was doubtful.

"No, I suppose I don't look much like an Arab now. I been here a long time, that's why. Can't hardly remember the Arab language even. But I looked like an Arab then, and I was, too. And I was lost in a sandstorm with five friends, and when it blew over we had lost our camels and water, and the heat was coming down like a hot hammer. Well, you can't last long like that out in the Sahara Desert, so soon enough we were stretched out flat on the sand, tongues swollen up like peaches in our mouths, all ready to die."

He fell quiet and I didn't encourage him. Better yet I should get some sleep, and I laid my head back. I popped my eyes open when he spoke next.

"Damn them goats! All friends, and they all died, every one of them, and it was my fault. I was the one who got 'em out there. All my fault. I told 'em we was going to be rich and famous, but they all died out there. One at a time they went, just one at a time, and it was bad. And it all started with them upside-down goats. You want to hear about that?"

I looked at him again. Could be, I thought to myself. Maybe he was in World War II. There were troops over in the desert. Maybe he really did get lost in the desert. Maybe he was shell-shocked or something, thinking he was an Arab and all. Who knows, maybe he was some sort of hero and gave up his mind for his country. The least I could do was be patriotic and listen to him for a while.

"Sure," I said. "You were lost in the desert."

"What's your name now?" the old bum asked me, putting the question in such a way that he would be happy with an alias if I had one. But I told him my real name. Then he told me his.

"Mine's Ali Azizi Abdurrahman Hafiz. Up north they call me Tex and down south they call me Bob."

"Doesn't anyone call you Ali?"

"You can call me Ali," he said, "but I'll answer to almost anything."

[9]

So Old Ali stretched out his legs and took a deep breath.

"Anyhow there we was lost in the desert, after that storm, and we was arguing with each other, losing our morale, you know. And this one fellow, he says it was all foolish in the first place. He believed that the King was alive and well, and that the Three Brothers was with him, hidden out somewhere. But then somebody else says the King was dead. He says that lots of people saw him stretched out stiff on that camel when they brought him in, and that the Three Brothers might be just over the next sand dune, waiting to be found. Now my opinion was—"

"Wait a minute," I said. "What's this about a King and Three Brothers? What happened to the goats? You were talking about goats."

"Huh? The King and the Brothers? Well, that's why we was out in the desert. You think we was out there on a picnic?"

"I don't know why you were out there. You didn't say. I never heard of the King or the Three Brothers."

"Never heard of them? Well, you would have heard about them if you lived over there. Everybody heard of them. They was famous."

"I wasn't even *born* yet."

The old bum looked at me blankly for a moment, then said, "Well, that's why we was in the desert, looking for the Three Brothers."

"All right. And a King was lost out there, too?"

"Nah," the old bum said. "The King was dead. Some said he was alive, but not me."

"Hold on," I said. "Why don't you tell me from the beginning? Who was this King? And what were you doing out in the desert?"

"Looking for the Three Brothers," Old Ali said. "Ain't that clear? Didn't I tell you that?"

"So they were lost, too, walking around out in the desert, and you and your friends were trying to find them?"

"Hell, no. They couldn't walk. They was brass trumpets, three of them, all hooked together on a golden chain, and they was out there somewhere in the sand, and whoever found them was going to be rich, and me and those five others was looking for them. Ain't you paying attention?"

"Well, forget it, then," I said, folding my arms and turning a bit to the side. He could do better than that. I closed my eyes, and with my head against the boards could feel the whole rumbling of the train come through my skull bone, down my neck, and into my backbone. Old Ali was quiet. Let the old bum talk or let him not. I wasn't going to be plucked along like that. When he spoke again, he made a proper beginning to the story.

The Story of the Three Brothers

"Once upon a time," said Old Ali, "there was a King, rich with gold. He had a palace and treasures and all the sorts of things a king can get."

"That's better," I said, turning my head slightly

and opening an eye at him. We were passing a row of trees, and the sun flashed in on him. He blinked at me and seemed to be smiling. I turned my jacket collar up for a thin pillow between me and the boards, closed my eyes, and listened. He began again:

"Once upon a time there was a King, rich with gold. He had a palace and treasures and all the sorts of things a king can get. This King ate the best food, and he had musicians to play for him, and slaves, and women, and gardens, and fine clothes, and everything a king might want. He could send around the world for something he wanted, and get it right under his hands. But one thing that he wanted he didn't have, and he couldn't buy it, but a sort of thing you can have even if you're naked and poor. What he wanted was wisdom, and he wasn't a wise man and he knew it. He wasn't a fool, you understand. He was smart enough to be a King, but he wasn't wise. He was sorry about this and wanted to change it. Now, there's some wisdom in that already, just wanting to be wise. So the King studied books and had teachers come to teach him, and he learned of stars and bugs and men and love. But for all he studied and for all he talked and for all he listened, he didn't feel any wiser than before.

"He would stand at his palace windows and look out at all the thousands of people walking about in the city, and it bothered him greatly to think that just any one of those people might get wisdom and be wise, and himself the King must always be poor in that. Yet there was one way he knew to get wise, and it was a quick and easy way. It was like this.

"In with all his other treasures were two brass trumpets hooked together on a golden chain. Once there had been a third one, but it was lost or stolen, no one knew when or where or how, and a piece of golden chain hung down where it was once attached to the other two trumpets. The three brass trumpets were called the Three Brothers. And each had his own name. The first one was named WHERE DID I COME FROM?, and the second was named WHO AM I?, and the third missing and lost Brother was named WHERE AM I GOING? And there was a legend about the Three Brothers, and a promise. Here's how it was.

"It was said that if any man could ever get those three brass trumpets together on the golden chain, and if those three trumpets were blown at the same time, there would come out a sound, a tone, a music such that the hearing of it answered the questions that make you understand WHERE DID I COME FROM?, WHO AM I?, and WHERE AM I GOING? That's a lot of wisdom, to know such things. And the man who knew such things would be very, very wise, perhaps the wisest man on earth. But it couldn't happen, because no one knew where the Third Brother was. Four Kings before this King had looked for the Third Brother but had never found him, and this King had looked for him, too. He had looked all over the world, and still had men in every kingdom and country asking about that trumpet, trying to search it out. The King was after wisdom and didn't care how much it cost him to get it. When his searchers found the Third

Brother they would know him, because all the Brothers had their names engraved on them, and the missing Brother might yet have a piece of gold chain hanging from him. But the King's men never found that missing trumpet."

Just then the train's engine blew its whistle, sounding like a gigantic and terrible owl. We rumbled over a road crossing. I took off a shoe and scratched down into my sock, still looking at Old Ali, nodding for him to continue.

"Now that city where the King lived wasn't far away from where I lived in the desert," said Old Ali. "And the first time I ever went to that city there was much talk about the Third Brother. A clue had been found that told something about how to find him. The King's teachers had found the clue in an old book, a strange old book with all the future and past written about in it, but strangely told, with poetry and sayings you had to think about, and wonder about. Secret things, you know, said in a way that not everyone could understand. And it was in that book where they found a little rhyme that nobody had ever noticed before. It was a big book with many words, and no one man could understand it all. But one man did find this little rhyme—and he understood that it must be about the missing Brother, and it went like this:

> Seek the Brother who is lost,
> from a man upon the brink,
> a man who'll never sin again,
> nor ever evil think.

[14]

"What would you make of that?" Old Ali asked me.

"Say it again," I said, for I like a riddle. I slipped my shoe back on while Old Ali repeated the rhyme.

"Hmm, that's a hard one," I said.

"And there's another part to it," said Old Ali. "It's a sort of curse. Listen:

> Some will die from water,
> swollen tongues within their heads,
> some with swollen tongues will live,
> and follow silver threads."

"That's even harder than the first part," I said, after giving it a minute's thought.

"Maybe," Old Ali said. "But I know the answer to that part because the answer *happened* to me. I didn't have to figure it out. The curse of it happened to me. See, it had to do with anyone searching for the Third Brother, or even all of the Brothers if they were lost. You remember how me and my five friends were lost out in the desert?"

"Sure," I said, "but last time you said that you and your friends *was* lost out in the desert."

"Well, we was," Old Ali said.

"Never mind," I said. "So there you was. Then what happened?"

"That's the point," Old Ali said. "See, we was out there, searching for the Three Brothers."

"But how did the Three Brothers get lost in the desert?"

"Listen to this first," said Old Ali. "It's all part of the same story."

I settled back and crossed my legs. The clean, fresh smell of wheat fields blew through the boxcar.

Death in the Desert

"All right, we were lost and had no water, and our tongues were swollen up, and after a while we just laid down in the sand. We stretched out, asleep and dying, sand all around us and miles from anyplace. But then, under that dreadful hot sun and out of emptiness, came a loud voice that woke us up. We all sat up and looked around, but there was no one in sight. We looked at each other, and the voice came again. It said just one word, that's all. It said, 'Smell.' Don't know where that voice came from, but just as it said that word a little wind came along, and on that wind we could smell water. We headed that way, and just over a sand dune was a little pool of water, glittering, more beautiful to us than a bushel stack of gold coins. We all fell down to drink. But we hardly got more than a swallow when one of my friends coughed, grabbed at his throat, and rolled over, dead."

"Poison water?" I asked.

"Not for the rest of us, just him. Strange how that was. We felt all right, and wanted to drink some more, but that little pool sunk into the sand, and we left that place. But since we'd had just the smallest taste of that water, we didn't walk very far before we were all dry again. Sand all around out there, far as the eye could see. Beautiful. Like a golden-white ocean. Beautiful if you have water and you're sitting up on a camel. But we were near dying again, and we laid down, not able to drag another step. Still lost, figuring we'd just go to sleep and die.

"But the voice came again and woke us up. It said just one word. 'Listen,' it said."

"Where did the voice come from?" I asked.

"Came from everywhere, nowhere. We didn't know. This was a long time ago. When you live in the desert you hear stories like that. You come to believe things like that can happen. So we listened, like the voice had told us to. And we heard water bubbling up close by. And right near there we found a little spring bubbling up into a little pool, and we fell down to drink. But we hardly got a swallow when one of my friends jumped up, cried out to Allah, and fell down dead.

"Then immediately the spring stopped bubbling and the pool sunk into the sand, and we started walking again, leaving our dead friend where he lay."

"Tongue swollen up," I offered, "like in the rhyme."

"Just like that," Old Ali said.

"And dying from water," I said, "like in the rhyme."

"Just like that. And we weren't much better off than before. The water didn't seem to last long with us. It was like drinking water in a dream. Still you wake up thirsty. Anyway, we didn't go far before we were laid out in the sand again. The sun was still right up there, pounding on us, and we laid down there to sleep or to die, whatever came first. Then the voice came again, talking out of nowhere. It said one word. 'Taste,' it said, and we sat there looking at each other, myself and my remaining three friends. We were beginning to see a pattern in this.

"Well, so we waited. And it seemed like that must have been the wrong word, because there was nothing to taste. We just sat there dumb for a while. Then I myself found the answer by accident. I had sand on my lips from laying in the sand, and I licked them. And when I did, the sand turned to little drops of water. So I took a desperate chance, scooped up a small handful of sand and threw it into my mouth. And I'll be darned, that sand turned to water when it touched my tongue and it ran cool down my throat. Then we all dumped sand into our mouths and it turned to water, except for one of us. He died in a terrible way—choking on sand. Then there was just three of us left, just me and two friends."

At this place in the story I was scratching vigorously at my stomach. Old Ali noticed my distraction and let the story drift out there with the blowing sand in the desert.

A Trumpet Is Taken from a Beautiful Woman

"Cuprex, that's what you want," he said. "Buy it at any drugstore. Comes in a little brown bottle. Good for cooties of any kind, scooters, scabbers, or inapoos. Hard to stop scratching at 'em once you start. Takes a strong mind. Builds character. Guess I never had much, myself. Always had to scratch—didn't know when to stop. Ambition, that's what it is. Always was ambitious. Wanted to be rich and famous, wanted to find something no one else ever found. That was my problem. But see where it got me—sitting out in the desert hearing voices and drinking dream water, and seeing my friends die off one by one."

"Yeah," I said. "Just like it said in that curse. How do you spell Cuprex?"

"Damned if I know," Old Ali said. "You got any water in that pack? Makes me thirsty talking about the desert."

"No," I said, "just clothes and things."

"You want to carry water with you if you're going to ride boxcars," he said, and he dug into his old bummy pack and came out with a bottle of water. He took a drink and handed the bottle over to me.

"Guys get locked in boxcars sometimes, get shunted off on a siding and die of thirst before somebody opens the door again."

I moved closer to him, took a drink, and handed the bottle back. In the light from the door, being closer to him now, I saw something in the curve of his nose, the darkness of his skin, his coal-black eyes. . . . Maybe he *was* an Arab. The train was up to a good roaring speed. We were traveling north. Golden wheat fields split the view with the bright blue sky. Tall grain elevators stood like giant silver torsos on the landscape. I turned the story over in my mind.

"So that solves that part of the riddle," I said. "If you hunt for the Three Brothers, you're cursed to die in the desert."

"That's pretty much it," Old Ali said. "Some live, but those other two friends of mine died, too. And it was more strange than the first three. Then there's the part of the riddle about the silver thread. You ought to hear that."

"But tell me first how the King found the Third Brother. And how did the Three Brothers all get lost out in the desert?"

Old Ali scraped up a handful of straw and held his hand out the door, letting the wind blow it away a little at a time, all the while nodding his head slowly, a faraway look in his eye. Then he turned to me.

"You know much about women?"

And when he said that I caught something in his eye, something I had seen just the night before in that flophouse. Two old men sitting on a cot next to mine talked about why they were so low down, how it had happened. One said it was strong drink, the other said it was a woman, and he had a look in his eye. . . .

"Young and beautiful," said Old Ali, looking out the door. He blinked, took out the rag of a red bandanna, and blew his nose. Then he coughed and looked at me again.

"What was I talking about?"

"I asked you how they found the Third Brother."

"A woman had it," Old Ali said, and he shrugged. "What else? A beautiful woman had it."

"Someone you knew?"

"Her? No, I didn't know her. How should I know her?" Then he picked up his red bandanna, wiped his nose, and looked at me under his brows. "Hah, you're a smart boy. But no, I didn't know her, not that one. Anyway, they solved that riddle and found the Third Brother. This woman I'm talking about had it, sort of a gypsy type for all you could tell, and she lived in a tent in a little oasis not far from the city, right under the King's nose, you might say, and he'd been looking all over the world for that trumpet.

"Oh, yes, she was young and beautiful. That's what they say. She kicked and screamed when they came to get the trumpet, and they had to fight her to get it away. And then when they took it a strange thing happened. Right before their eyes she started turning old, and she got gray and wrinkled and skinny, and her hair fell out and she couldn't stand up, and she fell down in a corner and cursed at them, and they left her there. They said she must have been two hundred years old."

"Did she keep getting old?" I asked. "Did she turn to dust right there?" I asked.

"An interesting idea," Old Ali said. "But I don't know any more about that. I guess she did finally, because she had to die, being so old she couldn't even get up off the ground, and getting older all the time."

The King Is Dead.
The Brothers Are Lost.

"What I do know is that the King now had the Three Brothers all together, and he was ready to hear them blow, and hear that music that would make him wise. But there was one more problem. The King didn't want anybody else to hear that music, because then they'd be wise, too, so it wouldn't be worth as much. Everybody being wise wouldn't be much different from everybody being dumb, that's what the King thought. So he had to hear those trumpets blow their music in secret, and all alone. He put in some time figuring out how this could be done, and here's what he did.

"He got together three musicians who could blow trumpets, and he put each of them on a camel. Then he got on a camel with the trumpets tucked in his saddlebag. He had one more camel with him and on that camel was sitting a big slave with a sharp sword. 'We'll take him along for protection.' That's what the King told the musicians just so they wouldn't get excited about anything. And that big slave was deaf and dumb, couldn't hear a sound or say a word, but the King knew signs to make to him so that he'd understand his job. Then they all rode into the desert, the five of them.

"Now, I guess you see what the King's plan was. The way he explained it to the big slave was by pointing to the three musicians and making a chopping motion with his hand at the back of his neck. The King was going to take everybody way out into the desert, far away from anybody, and then those three musicians would blow those trumpets, and the King would hear that music and become wise with knowing WHERE DID I COME FROM?, WHO AM I?, and WHERE AM I GOING? Of course, so would the musicians. But right then the King was going to make the sign for the head chopping to begin. And the King would come back to the city alone with his deaf and dumb slave, the wisest King of all Kings that lived in the world.

"So out they went into the desert. Everyone in the city waited. They knew the story about the Three Brothers, and they were proud and happy that they were getting such a wise King. It's a wonderful thing to have a wise King, a great comfort, because a wise King takes good care of his people. So they all waited, and feasted, and sang songs, and danced, and three days passed like a festival, waiting for the King to return, and there would be a greater celebration when he did return. They watched from the walls and the towers, watched out into the desert for the King coming back, wisdom and goodness just leaking out of him. Three days passed, then another day, then another. The singing and dancing stopped. Maybe the King was lost. Maybe they'd all got lost in the desert and died.

"On the next day a searching party was got together, and they was about ready to set out when a yell came from the towers. Way off in the distance, a cloud of dust was spotted. People crowded to the walls to watch. Camels were coming. Everybody made a great shout, but little by little the shout died down. Now they could see what it was. There were only two camels. And then they could see that something had gone very, very wrong out there in the desert.

"The big slave was riding the camel in front. On the other camel was the King, stretched out over the saddle. He was dead, and his stiff arms and legs bobbed up and down. They walked into the city through the high gate. The King was lifted off the camel and laid down on the ground. They looked at his face. He didn't look any wiser. There was not a mark on his body to show how he had died, and the Three Brothers were gone. They carried him into the palace.

"What had gone wrong? They couldn't understand it. They asked the slave what had happened, but he was deaf and dumb. He waved his arms around and pointed out into the desert, excited about something that happened out there, making motions and slobbering sounds, but no one could understand what he was trying to say. Finally everyone had to understand it the best he could. Some said this: some said that the three musicians blew the trumpets like they were supposed to, and the sound of all that wisdom, the sound of knowing that much, was too much for a man, and the King's heart had stopped, and that's how he died. And then, they said, the slave killed the musicians for thinking that they'd somehow killed the King. No, others said, that wasn't how it happened. What happened was that the King heard the trumpets

and the sound, and he got all that wisdom, and the slave killed the musicians, and the King decided to kill the slave just to make sure, but the King wasn't a young man and he dropped dead from trying, just natural. And others said, no, no, that wasn't it at all. Here's how it was: the musicians caught on that they were going to be killed, so they crept up on the King one night and smothered him, and then tried to kill the slave, too, but he killed them instead. And others said, no, it wasn't like that either. Listen, here's how it was. . . . And so forth. Believe what you want to believe. But here's the facts. The King was dead. The slave didn't bring the trumpets back. The Three Brothers were left somewhere out in the desert.

"So they tried to find out from the slave where they'd journeyed to. Which water holes did they use, and what stars did they sleep under? Where did he leave the Three Brothers? But the slave just waved his hands out there toward the sand. He didn't know, or couldn't tell. Didn't mean anything to him. He probably wasn't even thinking about the trumpets, didn't know anything special about them. He just let them lay where they fell, out there in the desert.

"So before the King was even buried, men were packing up and going out into the desert, some alone and some in groups, all looking for the Three Brothers. Well, what would you say they were worth? What would you say? Gems and gold? Why, you could have all you could ask for if you could find those Three Brothers, so searching in the desert was worth the danger of it. Some men returned to tell their stories about where they had looked, and the adventures they had, and some never returned, and the years passed, and no one found the Three Brothers. And always there were the sort of men who were ready to go out for another look, and young men almost always eager to go. The winds blow and the sands shift. And maybe they are just now laying freshly uncovered, three brass trumpets shining bright enough to be seen from miles away, hooked together on a golden chain."

Young Ali Tends Goats and Dreams

"And no one ever found them?" I asked.

"Not that I know about, and I don't think so. Because if a man was that wise the whole world would know about it. And I haven't heard about him. No. The Three Brothers are still out there, waiting to be found."

"And so you didn't find them either?"

"Nope, never did."

I thought awhile on the story. Old Ali scooped up another handful of straw and was letting it gently blow out of his hand, gazing far away across the wheat fields out the open boxcar door. I was wondering about the woman who had the missing trumpet, wondering how she got it, and how the riddle was solved that led the King to her.

"Who was the woman?" I asked, looking up at him, and once again he had that faraway look, letting the straw blow out of his hand, a going-away, a going-back look, and he spoke without moving.

"Sharon Bouquet," he said quietly. "A flower of the Mississippi, that's what I called her, and we was poor as stones, but . . ."

Then he jerked his head, said, "Huh?" and threw the rest of the straw out the door.

"Oh, her," he said, turning to me again. "Well, like I said, nobody much knew, just a gypsy sort and a robber to boot."

"And they found her by solving the riddle?"

"That's it, that's it. But nobody knew how they figured it out. Here it is again:

> Seek the Brother who is lost,
> from a man upon the brink,
> a man who'll never sin again,
> nor ever evil think.

It's difficult, sure enough. But listen, I think *I* figured it out all by myself, and it was real peculiar how that happened. Remember how I was telling you about those goats walking upside down in the sky?"

Here we were, back at the goats again. All right, so I'd have to hear about the goats. "Yeah," I said. "Upside-down goats."

"Well, like I say, that's how everything got started—those goats walking upside down in the sky. Here's how it was:

"Like I say again, I was born and raised in a tent in the Sahara Desert. There was me and my mother and my father, and we kept goats. A little tribe of us moved around together in the scrub desert, others keeping goats, too, and some brass workers, carpet makers, that sort of thing. Nomads we were, traveling around. Not much of a life, kicking goats around. Go to a little marketplace, buy, sell, trade. That was the sort of life. But I was young and I had other ambitions, dreamed dreams, and I was always thinking about other places I wanted to be. Nowhere to go out in the desert, not much to see, not much to do.

"But my father told stories about the big cities and marketplaces, and stories about big ships out in the oceans, and faraway places, and mountains and rivers. Then there were the old stories about lost cities, and mysterious caves, magic carpets, powerful genies, and about beautiful women who did things I could never understand, and I lived in those stories, dreaming and wondering about them most of the time. Goats? They might have lived in another world. I kicked them along and laughed a secret laugh at them, meaning that someday I was going to be off and gone to see all the wonderful things in the world, and I'd chase no goat ever again. That's how I felt. I wanted to get away from the life I had. For years I felt like that.

"All I was waiting for was a sign. That's the idea I had—must have got it out of a story. Sometimes there was someone in a story who had a sign given to him, then he knew what to do. The sign can be anything, and it's sort of like God telling you what to do, when it happens. And then you can't be wrong. So I waited for a sign. I knew it was coming and I waited for it, watching out for it.

"I kicked the goats along and looked out at the

horizon where the hot wavy air rose, and I saw things sometimes—like cities, mountains, lakes, tall towers, and great caravans crossing the desert. But those weren't signs, only mirages, and I knew that. And no sign came. By and by I got to laughing that secret laugh at myself, thinking I was just a fool, and I tried to be happy. But my heart was not with goats.

"So I had a fight with myself, trying to get my heart back, trying to make myself happy among those goats, and happy to take care of them like I knew I should. But it's hard fighting with yourself, deep inside, and one day I fought too hard and got sick with a fever, so I laid up in a dark tent, getting well. Three days I laid in there, sweating and tossing around, and on the third day my head was like being on fire, and I was struggling and sweating, coming awake and sleeping, hearing whistles and bells in my head, sometimes just laying there and moaning. And that's the day the sign came."

The Sign of the Goats

"I was half awake, laying there, and a little breeze came into the tent. I opened my eyes, happy for that little coolness. And there I saw it—right in front of my eyes—some goats walking upside down in the sky."

"Goats inside the tent?" I said.

"No. It was like this. It was just a *picture* of goats—on the wall of the tent, all in golden color, a picture of everything outside, the desert and the sky, and those goats walking upside down because the whole

picture was upside down, all the goats with their feet up in the air. I blinked at it, and just then a little wind came up again and the picture was gone. I was in the dark again. Well, I thought I was in real trouble. At first I thought that some angel, or some demon maybe, had come around to play games with me. So I rolled out of bed and got down to pray, expecting any moment I might be snatched up into the sky by my feet, left dangling there forever maybe, tending a bunch of upside-down goats eternally as some sort of punishment for not tending them properly when they were right side up. Anyway, I didn't know what it was and I didn't want any part of it. Scared the hell out of me, tell you the truth. I was your age and was in no mood to talk to any angel or demon, supposing one might pop up in a corner of the tent. I mean, how would you like to explain yourself to an angel or a demon?"

I shook my head.

"Me neither. So I prayed awhile. Then another little wind came and I opened my eyes to look, because that's how that thing had got inside the tent before, coming and leaving with the wind, wherever it was from, heaven or hell—and sure enough, there it was again, those goats walking upside down in the sky! Just a perfect picture there on the dark wall of the tent. And something else, too.

"When I'd got down to pray I'd raised some dust in there, and now I could see that the picture was shining out of a little tiny hole on the other side of the tent. Very strange. I crawled over there on my knees and put my finger over that little hole. The picture of the goats disappeared. I let my finger go, and there it was again. Now, this was amazing, and something I'd never heard about. Somehow, when the wind ruffled the tent, that little hole had come about just right to shine that picture on the opposite tent wall, a perfect picture of what was outside, but all upside down. It was a wonderful thing, and by poking at that hole I could make that picture come and go as I pleased."

"I see how it was," I said. "You can make a thing called a pinhole camera that works like that, too. At just the right distance it can project a picture all in focus, but upside down. The eyes work like that, too, turning pictures upside down on the other side of your eyeball. But in your brain you see it right side up."

Old Ali nodded. "That's what I know now. But right then I didn't know anything about that at all. For me, right then, I knew it was the sign I'd been waiting for. I saw that it was a natural sort of thing, but signs can be natural, and I crawled back in bed, trying to understand it. What could it mean? Mighty strange, that all the world outside, the desert and sky, the goats, could all be bunched up and shoved through a tiny hole, and then spread out again into a perfect picture. Signs don't always come plain and easy, I knew that, so I laid there working to understand it, and it was hard work."

Old Ali looked out the door then, and I followed his glance. We had come out of the great wheat fields now, and we were coming down off the Columbia plateau toward the Columbia River itself. Far off, I could see the hills and the cut shelves on the Washington side of the river, an ancient geography. The air was fresh, almost with a taste to it—the smell of the river.

"So here's what I thought," Old Ali continued. "It was a hard thought to get, and I believe the fever helped me, my brain being all warmed up and ready for some fast thinking, because the things I thought about went by so fast I still can't remember all of it, but it was perfectly good thinking. And how it came out was that I understood the meaning of the sign, and here's what it was.

"See, there are places in the world that are sort of like gates, sort of like doors, where everything you can see goes in and out. Some of these places you can find, like that little hole in the tent, but that's only a picture. But there are other places, invisible places, little gates, little centers like that hole, where life itself, the being and existence of things, you understand, is all crowded down like that, and out of those little centers life comes through and is spread out in all directions. Then, at last, of all those little places in all the world, there's one little gate, one little center where all the other centers come and go out of. And that place is the center of all the light and life and being of the whole world. That's what I thought—that there was a place that was the center of the whole world."

Old Ali took off his hat and scratched his head. It

was a hard thing to explain, I could see that, but he did it pretty good and I thought that if I had a fever I might understand it better. But there was more to come.

"That was a big idea," Old Ali said, putting his hat back on. "But a bigger one came right after that. It was all of a sudden like a bright light was shining inside my head, and I saw that not only was there a center of the world, but that there also had to be a center of the entire whole universe, a center where all the worlds and stars and the sun and everything shined out from, all of everything that existed, and it came to me hot and burning that this very place— the Center of the Universe—might be somewhere in the world itself. And then the meaning of the sign came to me—like a hundred brass gongs going off, like hot gold and silver being poured over my brain, came to me just as the wind came in again and those goats were there again walking upside down in the sky. It was a great holy moment. Because it came to me that the sign meant that it was myself, just a goat-herd, who was meant to go out and *discover the Center of the Universe!*"

A Visit with Old Abdullah

Old Ali had been sitting up straight, using his hands to explain all this to me, and now he slumped back against the boards and let out a long breath. I looked at him closely. What he said was crazy, but I could sort of understand it, too. He relaxed some, then spoke again.

"So that's why I was born," he said. "That's how I saw it. It was the reason for my whole life. My sign had come at last. I crawled out of the tent and laid on my back in the sun. The sweat dried off me and in another day I was well, and packed, and ready to leave home.

"I never felt so right about anything in my life. Everything I put my hand out to seemed to float up to me, and every step I took seemed to be measured out in heaven. Everything came so right and easy and perfect that I knew the sign was leading me, like God was making a pathway for me. Everything I saw and everything I thought and everything anybody said pointed right exactly at the sign, just proving it over and over again. All I had to do was walk out into the world, and nothing could go wrong.

"Of course my mother and father didn't want me to go. But I told them I'd come back rich and famous— because a man would be very rich and famous who first discovered the Center of the Universe, something so important as that. The discovery of America?— Why, that was nothing compared to what I was going to discover, and then the whole world would hold out its hands to me.

"My mother asked me to explain it one more time. —The Center of the Universe, I said, —where all things enter and leave, where everything comes together, where nothing moves and from where all

[37]

things spread out and start existing.

"My father said he had seen the center of the universe in a newborn goat's eye. My mother said she had seen it in the design on a carpet. But they understood about signs, and if I had one they knew it wouldn't do any good to argue with me, and they gave me their blessings, asking Allah the All Merciful and Compassionate, Guide of the Righteous, Protector of the Faithful, to be with me. And I left home. That very afternoon I left, and all before me was the desert, except for one single tent.

"An old man lived there named Abdullah. He lived by medicine, taking care of the feet of goats, camels, dogs, and people, making ointments and wrappings, a sort of doctor, you know."

"—God is great, he said as I passed his tent.

"—God is great, I responded, which is all very much like saying hello and good-bye as you're walking along and meet someone.

"But then Old Abdullah called me to come into his tent, so I ducked under the flap. He was sitting in the dim light of a small lamp, his water pipe by his side, a thin curl of smoke rising from it. He nodded, and I sat down on the carpet in front of him. I was all in a hurry to be on my way, but I had respect for old people, so I sat quietly while he smoked for a minute, looking at me. Then he spoke.

"—So at last before I die, said Old Abdullah, —I have lived long enough to know another who has had the vision.

"—The vision? I said.

"—The sign, he said.

"—Do you know about the sign? I asked, for I had told no one the sign, but only that I was going off to seek the Center of the Universe. I didn't suppose that anyone would have understood about the goats.

"—No, he said. —I don't know what your sign was. Men have different signs to lead them, different visions, but the way they point may be the same. Long ago I, too, had a sign that sent me out to seek the Center of the Universe.

"He picked up the stem of his water pipe then and puffed, and gazed at me. He smoked and was quiet, looking at me steadily, and the drifting smoke played about his wrinkled face, and he seemed for a second to be a younger man, and then just a boy, and then a man even older than he was. And for the first time since seeing the sign of the goats walking upside down in the sky, I felt small, and unsure of myself. I wondered about the cities I might visit, and the many thousands of people, and of mountains, and rivers, and of strange lands and customs, and of languages I didn't know. I remembered that I hardly knew about anything except goats, and I got disturbed, thinking of the richness and greatness of the world. I stuck a finger in a hole of my cloak and remembered that I was poor, and young, with no experience, alone, and I began to be frightened. Then Old Abdullah spoke again.

"—Do not be afraid, he said. —God smiles on you. But the world is wide and deep and dangerous to those who forget that they are held in the hand of the Almighty. And there are many who do not pray.

"He turned then and from a box at his side he took out a smaller box. The top was decorated with ivory set into the wood. He opened this smaller box and turned it upside down on the carpet between us, and several small objects fell out. Old Abdullah picked up one of these objects and held it up for me to see. I had never seen anything like it before.

"—This, he said, —is a shell from the ocean. Once a small animal lived in it in the dark kingdom of water where there are creatures with eight arms, soft all over like a camel's lips, without a bone in their bodies. And in those deeps also live creatures made of bone entirely with only two soft eyes to see. And monsters live there who could throw a shadow over a dozen tents if they swam in the air above us, and herds of fishes that number like a handful of sand. This shell is from that world. For hundreds of years it lay in those deeps so dark that the light of the sun could never reach it. But see how God has polished it to shine in the desert before your eyes. This is to remind us that God does not forget his creatures.

"He laid the shell down and picked up something else—a small dried flower, faint blue. He turned it in the light of the lamp and spoke.

"—This flower has lived in so high a place as that shell has lived in so low a place. So high a place that there's always snow, and it blows as thick as a sandstorm. So high is the place that you choke on your own throat because you don't have air, a place where it's colder than the deepest well is cold. But look here.

See how beautiful this flower is. See how it poked itself up and looked back at the sun? This is to remind us that the eye of God is everywhere.

"He put the flower down. Then he held up something else, and this thing was more strange than the others. What it looked like was a small stone, honey colored, clear and deep, and something shiny was inside it. I leaned forward and looked. Old Abdullah handed it to me. And inside this little stone was a small insect, a sort of beetle, shimmering purple, and I turned it in the light.

"—There are forests, said Old Abdullah. —There are forests of great trees you cannot imagine, they are so thick and tall, where animals as large as camels run free and wild with great figured horns on their heads. And many hundreds of other creatures, strange, some with needles all over their bodies, some with curved claws and green eyes that live in trees. There are furry creatures with bushy tails that leap from tree to tree, and thousands of different kinds of insects. And birds, hundreds of birds, all singing different songs, and animals that live under the ground, and always the great trees.

"—See this stone? It's called amber and is the blood of the great trees. One day a thousand years ago, or maybe a thousand thousand years ago, this blood from a certain tree bled and flowed over this beetle, and it hardened. And look! He is frozen in there until the end of time. See—his very last motion is there. See, those little feelers are frozen this very moment just as they were, waving in the air in his very last

moment thousands of years ago. There he is, there he always is, preserved by God. This is so we may remember to think on our deeds.

"I put down the piece of amber with the other things, carefully. Other objects lay there also: a pearl, a golden ring, a silver chain, a piece of quartz, some beads, a tiny bell, a chip of petrified wood. I gazed at these small treasures for a while, then looked up at Old Abdullah.

"—Have you really been to all those places in the world? I asked.

"He poked around the objects on the carpet, moving them about with his finger, and nodded. —When you go looking for the Center of the Universe, you must look in many places.

"Then he looked up and smiled at me.

"—But don't be afraid. God knows you, God is watching you, and God will take care of you. And I myself will do what I can to help you on your quest. Here.

"He picked up the piece of amber again and handed it to me. —This will bring you good luck. Keep it with you. Give it to no one. Never sell it, never lose it. When you return, you must have it with you. This is more important than I can tell you now.

"I took the amber and held it in my hands, and Old Abdullah put his hands over my hands and said, —God be with you. May he guide you and teach you. Remember to pray.

"Then he leaned back and took up his pipe. A cloud

of smoke drifted up over his face and I couldn't see him anymore, so I got up and left his tent."

The Robber

Old Ali stopped telling his story then. He took hold of the side of the door, leaned out and looked up at the sun, then leaned far out and looked up toward the front of the train, then down the line toward the caboose. Without saying anything, he pulled himself up and stood with his hand to the side of the boxcar, steadying himself.

He then moved out into the light in the center of the boxcar, turned about several times uncertainly, glancing out the door all the while as if he were searching for something, and finally got down on his hands and knees. He put his head down low between his arms, and his voice passed into a songlike tone as he said some words very rapidly, words in some language I didn't understand, high and bell-like, as devout and prayerful as I have ever heard, and I held my breath to listen. I was almost certain that I heard the words "orange blossom" and "midnight," but I might have been wrong. Anyway, they seemed to me to be very good words for a prayer. In a minute or two he raised himself up and got himself back to his place by the open door.

Looking doubtfully out the door, he shook his head. "Very hard to pray toward Mecca on a moving train. Don't remember all the words anymore, either, so now and then I put some special things in I think

God would like to hear. Wouldn't bother me any, if I was God." Then, making himself comfortable, he continued with his story.

"Now, that very night after leaving home I had my first adventure. Maybe God was teaching me, like Old Abdullah said He would, and He started right off with a hard lesson on that clear moonlit night.

"The first thing God taught me was that some men ride about at night on dark horses, and they wrap their faces up so no one can see who they are, and they wear dark robes and when you say, 'Praise Allah,' they don't say anything. That's the kind of man I met that first night away from home, all alone in the desert. He might have let me be, seeing how poor I was, but he didn't. He sat there on his horse after riding up to me, the silver fittings on his saddle glinting like sparks in the moonlight, and a brass trumpet hung alongside his thigh. Then he drew out a big curved sword, sitting way up there in the sky, with his horse snorting, and he told me to strip off all my clothes right down to the skin and hand everything up to him.

"Well, I thought if I told him how important I was, and what an important thing I was doing, that he'd show some respect, maybe just let me pass by. So I told him.

"—Hah, little fool, he growled, flashing his sword at me. —The Center of the Universe? Then perhaps I shall help thee in thy quest.

"He then threw back the garment that hooded his face, and only one stark, single eye glinted at me.

[45]

The other eye was put out, and a scarred black hole was there. The robber laid the point of his sword below the dark socket, and spoke.

"—Look into an emptiness that once was brightened by the sun, stars, beautiful women and flowers, and all wonder of the light of the day. Yea, a universe once lit this hopeless well, and even as this eye loved to see, so it was taken from me, taken by the point of a sword.

"Saying this, he thrust his sword toward my face and touched the point of it to my cheek, right below my eye.

"—Thou must know something of creation, little fool, if thou seekest the Center of the Universe.

"So saying, he raised the point of his sword an inch, and the point of it, sharpened to a needle's breadth, filled my vision like a great silver circle. The robber's voice then dropped to a heavy whisper.

"—Here is a question, little fool. There is a god of light who sits in the eye, and who makes creation. Yea, a god and a Center of a Universe, brightly illuminated. But with the smallest thrust of this blade I can destroy his bright universe. Tell me, then—thereafter does the god of the eye sit eternally in darkness, despairing and mad? Thereafter does the god of the eye make creation out of darkness? And what creation proceeds from madness and despair?

"The robber held the point of his sword steady. I blinked, and my eyelash touched it. I expected at any moment to be without an eye, and perhaps dead the next moment. But the robber spoke softly once again.

[47]

"—Such questions as this you will find at the Center of the Universe, little searcher, and thou mayest dread to find the answer.

"Then he laughed and whipped the sword away from my eye.

"—Little fool, I would give thee some answers to-night, but the moon lifts my heart somewhat, so let the mystery remain. And now be humble before this mystery, and stand naked before me.

"So I stripped off my clothes—what could I do? But in my right hand I held that piece of amber that Old Abdullah had given to me, remembering that it was important, though I didn't know why, and I handed up to the robber all my clothes and my pack besides. Then I was standing there naked, and he ordered me to stretch out my arms and open my hands.

"So very quickly I stuck that piece of amber into my belly button, and it held there tightly, and I stretched out my arms and opened my hands. He ordered me then to turn around, and saw that there was nothing more he could rob from me, and again he spoke in his curious, old-fashioned way.

"—Now, little mystery hunter, return naked to thy home and say that thou hast been lucky to see a mad creation ride away into the night, and hast yet lived. But I curse thee by the Horns of the Devil, little fool, and promise thee if ever again we meet I shall pierce thine eye, and then thou shalt know something of the Center of the Universe, and then thy fate shall be the same as mine.

"Then, after that parting curse, he flourished his sword, yanked at his horse, and galloped off, laughing and laughing.

"Then I was alone and shivering. A cold wind came up and I was standing naked in the desert. Remembering the piece of amber, I put a finger down to touch it. It at least was safe, nestled well and warm in my belly button. Perhaps it was a lucky charm. My eyes still saw, and I was alive. And I kept walking into the desert."

The Star Tent. Stolen Youth.

"Maybe I should have gone right back on home, but I would have been ashamed forever to do it, coming back the morning after I had left, after I had left all so proud and important, now coming back robbed and naked. So I kept on walking, and in about two hours I saw the glow of a fire. I came up closer and saw the light of a lamp inside a tent. Two camels were tied outside. And the tent was different from any I'd seen before, having a very large white star sewn on it."

Old Ali paused and shut his eyes for a moment, the better perhaps to see again in his mind this star tent of long ago. And the boxcar rumbled along. We made a wide turn and I caught a glimpse of the Columbia River. What if we turned west, back toward Portland, when we reached the river? I had been collecting straw to put under my seat for a pillow. There seemed no way to sit comfortably, and now I had just left my belt unbuckled so I could scratch more often and more freely. Well—so if the train was going to Portland? I'd be home for dinner and my good soft bed. In a few days I could get ready for a better start. Maybe that would be best. Old Ali started talking again.

"Now, an Arab is modest, and I was fretting about being naked, standing outside that tent. But the chill of the air made me call out at last. An old man came to the opening of the tent, looked at me, then went in and got a blanket.

"The tent belonged to this old man and his wife. They were on a pilgrimage to a holy place, and I was welcomed in the name of the Most High, and everything was made easy for me. They wrapped me up warmly and gave me strong sweet coffee to drink, and bread and cheese to eat. The old woman poured hot water into a basin, and I soaked my feet while I told them about the robber. I told them how he had threatened me, and how he had taken everything from me. They shook their heads in sympathy. They were very old, older than any people I'd ever seen. The woman didn't wear a veil, as is allowed for very old women. The coffee with thick sugar warmed me and made me bold. Now that the robber was far away, I began to play a brave part, and I said that if I'd had a sword and a horse, things might have come out differently, and I told how the robber had pointed his sword at my face and promised to stick me in the eye next time we met.

"—You are lucky to be alive tonight. Allah be

praised, said the old man, musing a bit. —Even stones have hearts, some say.

"—You wouldn't say it if you'd seen him, I said. —He showed me his ugly face and cursed me by the Horns of the Devil before he rode away, laughing and laughing.

"When I said that, the old woman gasped and put a hand on her husband's arm. He glanced at her, covered her hand for a moment, and stood up. He had a knife at his belt, as all Arab men carry in the desert. He put his hand on it and went to the opening of the tent. He stood there for a while looking out, then came back to his place. He patted his wife's hand, and looked at me again.

"—Was he alone, this robber? Was there a woman also?

"—Just him, I said.

"—What did he look like?

"—Well, it was night, you know, but he was a young man. Oh . . . and he had just one eye, and he had a trumpet hanging at his side.

"The old woman leaned a shoulder against her husband, and he put an arm around her.

"—Have you heard of him? I asked.

"—We know him, said the old man. —Yes, we have been robbed by him, too, and we have heard the same curse that he cursed you with. We also have been cursed by the Horns of the Devil.

"The old woman poured some more coffee for all of us. Her wrinkled hand was shaking. Her husband spoke again.

"—You say this robber was a young man, but he is not. Perhaps he is the oldest man on earth, and you may give thanks to God that he didn't take more from you than he did.

"I reflected on this and didn't see how he could have, since he took everything I owned, except for that little piece of amber, but I was quiet and listened to the old man, moving my feet in the basin of water and sipping my coffee.

"—That robber you met is over two hundred years old, said the old man. —And he has a wife who is also that old, for they have learned how to steal the youth of others. Once, when they were young, and loved their youth, they stole a charm which, used in the proper way, could keep them young always. No one knows what this charm is, or how it works, but with it they can steal the youth of others. They are wicked, both of them, and they have killed, and they are afraid to go to God, so they live by that charm and are always young.

"—Every few years, when they see the first gray hairs in their heads, when they see the first wrinkles in their faces, they go out riding with that charm and hunt for a young couple to steal their youth away from them. When they do this, a great age is laid upon the couple they steal from, and the robber and his wife ride off in their fresh, stolen youth. Yes, if he spoke to you of time, you have heard a master talk on the subject.

"The old man took his wife's hands into his, and continued his story.

"—Three years ago we met this robber and his wife. Three years ago I was only twenty years old and my wife less than that. On our very wedding night we met them, for we were traveling in the desert to visit my wife's ailing mother, who could not attend the wedding. And it was not far from this place that we met those two robbers.

"—We had not gone to bed yet when they came upon us quietly. The man cut his way into the tent (it has been mended with that white star you see) and his wife followed. Both had drawn swords, but they seemed not to want to kill us. They walked around us, and behind us, and held a lamp to our faces and studied us as one might study a horse, or cattle, as buyers do.

"—Then at last the man turned to the woman, and she nodded her head. She went out, and her husband followed after her. But at the door, this robber, he with the one eye, pointed his sword at us and cursed us by the Horns of the Devil, and told us not to move, not to come to the door, but to sit absolutely still until we heard them ride away on their horses. We were pleased to do just that, and so we waited, holding each other.

"—Then he was gone, and we waited to hear the horses ride off. We heard them mount their horses. And then we heard a horn blow, a long, wailing sound, and sitting there we seemed to go far away, out of ourselves, and then to slowly come back. And when we came back to ourselves, we heard horses riding off in the distance. We looked at each other then, and these are the faces we saw.

"The old man reached out for the nearby lamp. He held it between himself and his wife, so that their faces were well lit. They were very wrinkled, crowned with white hair, and their eyes were dim with a great age. Setting the lamp back down, the old man took his wife's hands in his, and they looked into each other's eyes. They seemed to forget that I was there. And in that moment their eyes were young again.

"—So you have come out here to find that robber, I said. —You're going to hunt and kill him for what he did to you?

"—No, said the old man. —I have told you. We are on a pilgrimage to a holy place. We must only pass this way.

"—Ah, I see. You go to ask God that you may have your youth back again.

"—No. We go to thank God for our love. Each year, in this month, we go to give thanks that our love was not taken from us as well. As for our youth that was stolen from us, let God do as He pleases.

"—Then you will never be young again?

"—It is said that when the charm is taken from those robbers, both the man and the woman will become their true and great age, and will go to God to be judged for their sins. And those they have stolen from, if they are still alive, will have their youth restored. The old man shrugged. —Yet no one finds them, no one captures them, and no one knows what the charm is. But old or young, we will make this pilgrimage each year until we die.

"The old woman prepared a place for me to sleep, and the old man found some clothes for me and set them out for the morning. Then we all went to bed, and I lay looking at the great white star from the inside of the tent. I touched the piece of amber still tightly held in the flesh of my belly. Then the lamp was put out, and I slept, remembering to give thanks to God that I was young."

In the City.
The King Solves the Riddle.

I interrupted Old Ali here.

"That horn, that trumpet the robber had—that was the Third Brother, the WHERE AM I GOING? Brother. It was, wasn't it?"

Old Ali nodded, but raised his hand for silence and continued:

"In the morning, they told me the right way to the city. They wished me the blessings of Allah, and I wished them the same, and as I left they gave me some bread and cheese and water to last me until I reached the city.

"I walked another day across the desert and slept on the open sand at night. I walked the next day too, and on the afternoon of that day I entered the tall gate of a great city.

"And what a city! What a place it was! You'd need a hundred eyes to see all there was to see—so many people all so busy, so frantic, running about, buying and selling and trading, bumping and pushing each other. You'd need a hundred ears to hear all there was to hear—the shouting and yelling, the crying and moaning, begging and whining, cursing and laughing, merchants gabbling, the rich yelling out orders, the poor grumbling out complaints, animals grunting and barking and bellowing, stomping and pounding all around like a thousand drums, leather beating on leather, metal banging on metal, and noise all about as thick as the air. And the air as full of strange smells as a stew thick with spices, the smell of cooking food everywhere, and the animal smell, dung smell, people smell, dust, smoke, perfume and garbage smell, all blended together in the great clatter of this living pot of a city. If the Center of the Universe was any-where on the earth, surely there could not be a better place to begin looking for it, so I thought.

"I bounced along, rump, belly, and head, knocked from shoulder to shoulder in those narrow streets, and in the shouting and trampling I found that I was joining right into it with a steady sort of tone coming out of my mouth all the time as if I were in a great living and singing chorus. And after the quiet desert I was glad to be there in among all the noise and people. I watched and listened and smelled and touched everything I could, wanting to learn all that God had to teach me, trying to remember everything, and all the time looking everywhere for another sign, for another clue to where in all this great moving body of people I might find the Center of the Uni-verse.

"But I had to eat, so I got a job with a barrel maker, splitting staves, and in the evening he gave me three coins, some cooked vegetables in a bowl, and a corner to sleep in. All the next morning I carried water for a blacksmith and worked his bellows for him until my arm was about to fall off, and he gave me some money also.

"At noontime I got some hot meat from a raggedy man sitting next to a little open fire, and I ate from my greasy hand and let myself be swept along the streets, going along wherever I was pushed, like a leaf in a rushing stream, and I let it carry me where it was going, coins jingling in my pocket and my belly full, eyes and ears wide open to everything and welcome to it, filling myself up entirely with the life of the city, looking for a sign, knowing a sign would come, wondering how anyone could possibly want to live in the desert and keep goats."

"Here was life and death. Here was a newborn baby at a corner, all wrapped up and being loved and fed, and around the corner was an old woman, starving, pulling her old legs along and holding out a hand for help, which nobody seemed to notice. Down a narrow alley I saw someone being beaten, maybe even killed, but what could I do? The screaming faded as I walked past, and a woman in a window said a kind word to me, then she looked at me in a peculiar way and said some puzzling things and I walked on, nearly walking into a dogfight, and I saw a thief steal another man's purse, and a man who could make a snake dance, and a young boy who could walk on the edge of a sword.

"And when the great noise of the throng now and then settled to a murmur, for even great noises have lulls, the murmur was about a riddle, and little by little I learned the story about the Three Brothers, which I have told to you. And the murmur said that the King had solved the riddle, and that the Third Brother would soon be found."

Old Ali held up a finger at me.

"Now, do you remember how the riddle went? I'll say it again:

> Seek the Brother who is lost,
> from a man upon the brink,
> a man who'll never sin again,
> nor ever evil think."

"Yes," I said. "And then there was a second part to it also. About dying from water, and swollen tongues, and a silver thread."

"True," said Old Ali. "And you know something of what that meant, myself and those others dying out there in the desert. But the part of it I've just said, that first part, was the part that was solved by the King, so it was said. And the people were excited, for soon the Third Brother would be found—and the King would get great wisdom. So a festival was brewing in the city, and when I heard of the riddle and the Three Brothers it was all just more of the wonder of the city to me. I let myself be swept along in the flood, and I was happy with it all, and I thought that God was good."

An Execution.
A Promise Is Kept.

The train had reached the river. We turned east, away from Portland. I wondered where I'd sleep this night. Perhaps in the boxcar. In case of that, I had a heavier jacket in my pack. Tomorrow I'd have to get work. At least I could wash dishes for a day or two. The sun was high, and the sparkling Columbia made me feel hopeful. Old Ali continued:

"Then the movement of the great body stopped, and I found myself in a big circle of people standing around an open place, a large square. I let the press of the bodies squeeze me up to the front of the circle until I was standing looking across this empty square. Maybe the King was about to come out to announce the solution to the riddle, or perhaps a Prince was visiting, or something anyway was about to happen that was very rich or very royal. For all around the circle were men dressed alike in broad black sashes and tall boots, dressed in flaring yellows and reds. They were some sort of guards, I supposed, King's men perhaps, and they were keeping the people from pushing forward into the square. And a laughing man was allowed to dance around the inside of the circle, juggling balls and collecting coins.

"Oh, what a place was this city! Was there no end to the color, the sound, the thronging, the wonder of it? Was every day such an entertainment, such a carnival? But it wasn't a carnival at all, what was about to happen, yet something maybe of an entertainment, if you like that sort of thing.

"And now came a great shout from the far side of the circle and the people parted, and through that pathway held open by the guards out walked a man in a green cloak. And behind him came a big, half-naked, slavelike man, with a wide sword in one hand and a rope in the other. And on the other end of the rope was a man walking with his hands tied behind his back, his head held down. Behind him was one of those guards, pushing him with a stick, who now and then hit him on the back, and in the neck, so that the man was all stooped over from the pain.

"There were other guards also in the group, and well-dressed, important-looking people. But the sleek man in the green cloak seemed to be the most important of all. They came to the center of the square and stopped. And where they stopped—I saw it for the first time—there was a chopping block. The slave with the sword took that poor man on the rope, grabbed him by the hair, and shoved his head down onto the block and held it there until the man stopped moving. Then he stood back and looked at the man in the green cloak. Out from under the cloak a hand crept, a ring on every finger like a jeweled snake, and he raised one single finger and let it fall. It was a small enough motion to end a man's life. For at that signal the half-naked slave raised his sword and brought it down and chopped the man's head off. The head fell to the sand, rolled a little, and stopped."

"Not really?" I said. "Did you really see that happen?"

"Well, and what happened next was worse," said Old Ali, and he took a deep breath and continued.

"When that head stopped rolling, the man in the green cloak grabbed its hair in his hand, rings shining on every finger, and he lifted the dripping head up off the ground. He then put his lips up to the thing's ear and said something to it. Then he turned that chopped-off head to *his* ear, and put his ear up close to its lips and made like he was listening, like the head was talking to him. And the whole crowd gasped."

"No!" I cried. "It didn't talk. It *couldn't* have talked."

"I don't know," said Old Ali. "I won't say I saw that head's lips move, and I won't say I heard anything, but the crowd gasped and hushed down absolutely quiet when this was happening. And in the quiet, the man in the green cloak listened with his ear up to the lips of that chopped-off head, and his face looked like he was hearing something, and he nodded. He nodded his head up and down, slowly, like he was hearing and understanding. It was a horrible thing to see—but I myself, of all that crowd, had seen something more horrible still."

Old Ali moved a little in his seat then and dug into his back pocket. He took out his bandanna and rubbed it across his forehead and around his neck. He wiped his lips and stared for a moment at the floor. I waited. What could be more horrible than a man pretending to talk with a chopped-off head?

"Now, all before this time," Old Ali continued, "that beaten man had held his head down and I hadn't seen his face. But now that head was held up full face toward me, and it was the very head of that robber who had robbed me in the desert. One eye was a dark hole, and the other eye was open and staring right at me, and it glinted with its last film of moisture, glinted as I had seen it glint along the edge of the sword. It was the robber who told me that next time we met he'd pierce my eye, and that then I would know the Center of the Universe.

"And as I saw this and recognized the head, the man in the green cloak listened to that chopped-off head, and nodded, and the glinting dead eye stared at me, piercing me like the point of a sword into my eye, and a cold sweat dashed across me and I fell down in a faint.

"For a long while all was deep and empty darkness, but then I must have passed into sleep, for I had a dream. I dreamed I was home again and in a dark tent, and I saw goats walking upside down in the sky, and I dreamed of that tiny hole in the tent, and in my dream I got down and put my eye up to it, and the hole changed to the point of a sword. Then came a foul smell to my nose, and a foul taste in my mouth like blood, and I was no longer looking at the glinting point of a sword, but I was face to face and staring into the eye of a chopped-off head, and the head, floating in the air, nodded at me, and then it began

laughing and laughing. I kicked my feet violently and came awake with a scream.

"I was sitting next to a building where someone had dragged and propped me. The square was filled with people now, all going about their business, children laughing, dogs barking, buying and selling and shouting, feet tramping about. I was shaking all over and hardly had the strength to stand up. The chopping block was now gone from the square, and the blood was all mixed up in the sand and forgotten. Staying next to the walls, I moved from building to building, trying to get far away from that place, trying to find a gate that went out of the city. I didn't want to hear any more of the city, or see any more, or smell any more, or touch anyone anymore. I wanted to get out where there was just sand and sun and sky, where it was clean and quiet. And when anyone caught my eye, it was like seeing the dead eye of the robber, and it seemed that strangers were nodding at me as I passed along. I was lost, and ran around next to the buildings like a rat, afraid to talk to anybody, afraid to look at anybody, and finally I saw a big gate and I ran out into the desert in a panic. Because now it all came clear to me. I had found the Center of the Universe, just as the robber said I would, when next we met. The promise was kept."

"But how?" I asked. "What did you find? I don't understand."

Old Ali smoothed the dust in front of him with the palm of his hand.

Crazy Thinking

"I had thought that to find the Center of the Universe would be like a blessing from heaven," said Old Ali. "But instead it was like the robber's curse, come out of hell." And in the smoothed dust between his legs he made two dots with his index finger.

"See—a person's eyes are the answer. See—the eyes are like that little hole in the tent, because everything in the world comes in through your eyes and makes pictures in your head. So the eyes are like gates, like small centers of all that is real and spreads out beyond, like the hole in the tent. That dream had made me know it. But more. Here is the question. Do the world and the universe and all existence come *into* the eyes, or do they go *out* from the eyes? It's a question about creation. Then I remembered how the robber had said that a god sits in the eye. And the answer came to me like an inspiration. The sharp point of the eye of the dead robber had pierced me, had told me what now came to me perfectly clear and true. It is all an illusion that the world and existence come into the eyes. It is just the opposite, and I understood. All existence goes *out* from the eyes—all existence is the creation of the brain and the mind. I had found the god who sits in the eye. I had found the Center of the Universe—and it was me."

For a minute we sat silently. I stared intently at Old Ali, and he stared into the dust at those two dots he had made, and blinked his eyes.

"But, but . . . that's not true," I said. "That's . . ."

"Crazy," Old Ali concluded for me, heaving his back against the boards. "Sure, I was crazy. It was the shock, you know, and the coincidence of everything. You know, it's sort of like being God, being the Center of the Universe, and everything that happens . . . well, that's all just part of yourself, if you know what I mean. But when you're crazy, how would you know it? I couldn't tell the difference. Seemed perfectly natural to me. And remember—there was more to that robber's curse. Remember—he also told me that when I knew the Center of the Universe, when my quest was done, then my fate would be the same as his."

I nodded.

"Way back in those days we believed in curses, and now that the curse was half completed, the last of it would be that my head would be chopped off, the same as the robber, and I expected it to happen soon. From what I'd seen of the city, it seemed to me that just anything might happen. So there I was in the desert, running scared away from that city, away from people, thinking that I would be snatched up for whatever reason, for whatever mistake, and dragged to a chopping block. Why not? Who cared? A curse was working on me. It seemed the easiest thing in the world that I could have my head chopped off. Maybe that's just exactly the thing that happens to people who find the Center of the Universe. In a way, you know, it even seems sort of right, and in a way, you know, it seems almost like a relief, getting your head chopped off after you have that sort of inspiration. But I wasn't ready for it. So there I was, running off into the desert, crazy and terrified."

"You don't believe all of that anymore?" I said.

"All of this was a long time ago," Old Ali said, and he sighed. "But it's a long question, and you never get rid of ideas like that entirely, even when you know it was all crazy, but you learn to live with it. See—I know I'm on a boxcar, and I know that you're sitting over on that side, and the sun is shining and the river is flowing out there, and if I close my eyes or die or disappear it will all be the same. But still . . . Well, once you get an idea like that, once you believe you're the Center of the Universe, once you go that crazy . . . Well, I think about God a lot, and that's what's left of it, and wondering. . . ."

Old Ali whisked his hand in the dust in front of himself, stared out the door for a minute, then looked back at me.

"But let me tell you what happened next. I almost died out there in the desert, stumbling around, not caring where I was going. But a caravan found me and took care of me. All the time I kept my eyes closed and wouldn't talk. I had the idea that people could *see* that I was the Center of the Universe. And next would come the head chopping, you know. So I played like I was blind and dumb. I slipped away from the caravan and the next day almost died again, but a man with camels loaded with jars found me and took care of me. That night I ran away from him, too. I walked all night under the stars, and very early in the morning I knew where I was. Somehow by accident I came upon a group of tents, and I was home. But I couldn't go home like I was. I was afraid to see anyone, even my mother and father, and I decided just to pass on by and keep dying out there in the desert where it was flat sand, sky, and stars, nothing else."

Old Abdullah Reveals the Center of the Universe

"Then I saw Old Abdullah's tent, and there was a light inside. And I knew I wanted to tell someone all about it, and I thought he'd understand. Maybe I wouldn't have to die. Maybe he could hide me, and I was hungry anyway, and thirsty, and sore, and I wanted to sleep. So I went up and into his tent. I told him everything, the best I could, even crazier than I tell it now, shaking like a little tree. Then I asked him to let me hide in his tent and never come out except at night, and I'd do any work he wanted, but just let me stay there, and I'd never be any trouble, and I expected to die before long anyway. Just let me stay there in the dark so nobody would ever know about me and come to get me and drag me off to a chopping block. I promised him I'd die soon, or go out into the desert again, but just let me stay for a while and sleep. And then I started crying, and I laid down on my face on the carpet, shaking and sobbing.

"Old Abdullah had listened to all of this quietly,

while he just smoked and watched me. And now, as I cried for ten minutes, he just sat there smoking and didn't say a word. Then at last I was all out of tears, and, taking his silence for a response, I started to crawl out of his tent into the desert again. But then he spoke.

"—Well, now, said Old Abdullah. —Who would have thought that the Center of the Universe could be so shaken? Who would have thought that the Center of the Universe could tremble so? I would have expected it to be firm and solid. And who would have thought the Center of the Universe could be so humbled? I would have expected it to be upright and straight, brave and confident, being so important as all that. What? Talk about dying, and hiding? Do you suppose the Center of the Universe is worried about dying and trying to hide itself away somewhere?

"Then he chuckled. And how could he? Here I was, laying at his feet, broken and crying, and he was laughing. . . . But it was only for a moment, and softly. Then he spoke again.

"—Remember that when you left here I gave you something to take with you, to hold on to, never to lose? Did you remember that much, or did robbers and the city steal it from you?

"I remembered, but I hadn't thought of that piece of amber for days. I didn't even know if I still had it. I put a finger to my belly button, and it was still there. I took it out, and Old Abdullah took it from my hand. He held it up and turned it in the light of a candle.

"—When I was your age, he said, —I too went out looking for the Center of the Universe. I went all around the world looking for it, and I saw many things, and I saw death, too, and suffering, and birth and joy. And also many lies tried to get into my mind, and also crazy ideas, but I prayed to God and he protected me, and I kept my mind and I kept looking. And finally I myself found the Center of the Universe. And this is it.

"So saying, he turned the piece of amber in the candlelight. I stared at it, the shimmering purple beetle in the honey-colored stone, stared like I was hypnotized. Fire, stone, gold, iridescent purple beetle, all these days riding in my belly. Then Old Abdullah closed his hand over it, took out the small box where it had come from when I first saw it, and put it in with the flower, the shell, and those other objects, and closed the lid of the box.

"—Do you understand? Old Abdullah asked. —Because you had that piece of amber with you, always very close to you, I thought you'd find it out for yourself. The Center of the Universe was always with you. But you made a mistake in thinking it was yourself. I'm sorry you thought the Center of the Universe was yourself—that must be very hard to bear. It was a close guess, but wrong. But now it's come out all right anyway, so put it out of your mind. The Center of the Universe is not you. No one wants to harm you. Go home now, and be at peace.

"So I went home, not exactly at peace, but not nearly as crazy as I had been. And after a while I even stopped worrying about having my head chopped off."

Old Ali then laid his back against the boards and gave a great yawn and stretch, shook his shoulders, reached inside his bummy pack, and took out his bottle of water. He took a drink and handed it to me.

"Ahhhhhhhh," he groaned, stretching again. "Any food in that pack of yours?"

I shook my head.

He reached in his pack and brought out a little scrap of newspaper with nuts wrapped inside it, and set it between us. I scooted up, and we sat closer, chewing nuts, a mixed variety.

"Pick fruit," he said. "Eat all you can, buy nuts with your pay. You can live like that. Drink milk, eat some beans, and you got all you need. Try Yakima—peaches, cherries, apples. Of course, you can work in the cannery, but they keep an eye on you there. And it's inside work, no place for me, but you might like it. Drink some more water if you want."

I was looking at him, and thinking that he was indeed old—maybe ninety even. But could these stories be true? Was he really an Arab? Tex? Bob? But maybe he *had* lived in the Sahara Desert. And the stories might have happened to someone, if not to himself. But maybe he *believed* they happened to him. Maybe something had made him go crazy, and this was the result of it, these stories he was telling. But yet . . . could it be true? I took a drink of water.

"And so the Center of the Universe is a beetle in a piece of amber?" I said.

"It's something to think about anyway," Old Ali said. "And I was happy to hear it. It got me to thinking, too, about how all that business with the robber was just a coincidence, just a lot of crazy chances. Because it's coincidence that can drive a man mad. Why—no man is so sane that a half-dozen chances, well selected by the Devil or whatever, might not drive him crazy. Then when you *get* crazy, there's nothing that doesn't mean something, if you follow me."

I didn't, but shrugged in a knowing way and chewed my mixed nuts.

Thinking No Evil

"So I tended the goats again and wondered a lot about all that, and I thought about that trumpet the robber had, and about his wife, and about that old couple in the star tent, and about that riddle that was the clue to how the Third Brother could be found. You remember how that went?"

I did, and having heard it three times before, I could recite it.

> "Seek the Brother who is lost,
> from a man upon the brink,
> a man who'll never sin again,
> nor ever evil think."

"Exactly," said Old Ali. "And thinking about all the things that had happened to me, I figured out what it meant. The problem of it is, the riddle says you could find the Third Brother by asking a man who will never sin again or even *think* an evil thing. Now, that's impossible. Sure, there are good men, even saints, who never sin, who never do evil things. But thinking? Well, thoughts blow through your head like a wind, and like the wind carrying leaves, you don't know what it might carry through your head. And so some thoughts that blow through your head, some of the things a man thinks, have *got* to be evil. It can't much be helped. That's how a man is, even if he's a saint. You've got to be dead to stop thinking evil things, even if you don't do them.

"So there's the problem. That rhyme says you've got to find such a man, one who'll never think evil things again, and ask him where the Third Brother is. But there is no such man."

"But they found the Third Brother," I said, scratching a leg and thinking outright evil thoughts about whoever left those lice in that bunk I'd slept in.

"They did. So the King or his men *did* solve the riddle, and so did I finally. How it came to me was like this. One day I watched my father cut a chicken's head off, and the bird ran a few steps before it fell over. Have you ever seen a thing like that?"

"I've heard of it," I said.

"Well, it happens. And so I thought about it and came to an understanding. See—there's just a small quick place, a sort of brink of time where there's a difference between getting killed and being dead. And see—maybe a chopping block is a sort of brink, too, like it's mentioned in the riddle, if you look at it that way. So here was my idea, and I believe it was the

King's idea, too. If you chopped a man's head off and spoke into his ear very quick and asked him the question about where the Third Brother was—maybe there was just time enough so he'd tell you the answer, and then he'd be dead so quick (well, he was dead anyway) that he'd be past all his evil thinking."

Old Ali held his hands out, palms up, as if this were all very simple to understand. But who could believe it?

"And that robber just happened to be the one you met? And he just happened to know where the Third Brother was?"

"It's an amazing thing, but it's true," said Old Ali. "And I'd gone crazy by the coincidence of it all. Had nothing to do with me or the Center of the Universe. That robber just happened to be caught at the time I was in the city, and he was the one they were going to try to get the answer from—where the Third Brother was—after they chopped off his head. And of all the men they might have tried, this robber was just exactly the one who really knew. And his one dead eye staring at me, and the man in the green cloak nodding his head . . . nothing to do with me at all. And when I finally realized this, I was done with the worst of that craziness I'd gotten into."

"But did the head actually talk?" I asked.

"Who knows? All I know is that they found the Third Brother right soon afterward. Remember how they took it away from that woman, and how she grew old right away? Wasn't that the robber's woman, and wasn't that the Third Brother? It was the sound of that trumpet that let them steal people's youth, the sound of that trumpet blowing his own name—WHERE AM I GOING, WHERE AM I GOING, WHERE AM I GOING? Anyway, that's the way I got it finally all figured out for myself."

More Death in the Desert

Old Ali then moved closer to the door and stuck his head out into the wind. We were passing farms and orchards now. He put a hand on his hat and his beard blew back over his shoulder.

"Coming up to Pasco soon," he said. "Gets hot in Pasco. You might like it better up toward Yakima."

But I was thinking about the Three Brothers, still. This was all getting to be a little too much to believe. Yet there was nothing Old Ali said that couldn't have happened. I followed the thread of the story backward, and it was logical enough, not just crazy babbling, and I thought back to the upside-down goats, and about Old Ali being lost in the desert with his friends, and that was a thread of the story that hadn't been picked up for a while.

"So when you felt better in your mind, you decided to go look for the Three Brothers yourself?"

"That's right. It was a couple of years later. Lots of people were out there looking for them. So like I told you, me and five friends decided to give it a try. Somehow I got this idea that I was the one to find them—since I was so mixed up in that story, you know. So off we went, and I already told you how three of them died."

"Yes, that voice came out of nowhere, and those three died from the water you were led to."

"That's it. And the other two died next, and then . . . Well, what happened then was the end of that riddle entirely. Remember how the last of it went?

> Some will die from water,
> swollen tongues within their heads,
> some with swollen tongues will live,
> and follow silver threads."

"I remember that," I said.

"And you remember how that third friend died from putting sand in his mouth and choking on it?"

I nodded.

"So there was nothing to do but leave him and go on our way, leave that place where the sand could magically turn into water. We kept going in the sun until once more we had to lay down again. But now we had some hope, and we weren't too surprised when that voice came again and woke us up. Three times it had saved us already, but we still couldn't see any-one anywhere. And this time the voice said, "Touch." Well, touch what? We touched the sand, we touched our noses, we touched each other. Nothing happened, no water came any sort of way. Then we saw it.

"Don't know how we didn't see it before, but right there just a little ways off was a hand, the hand of a man sticking out of the sand. But it was a gigantic hand, as tall as a man, all the fingers spread out and the thumb stuck out, and it was made of solid brass.

"We walked up to it, myself and my two friends,

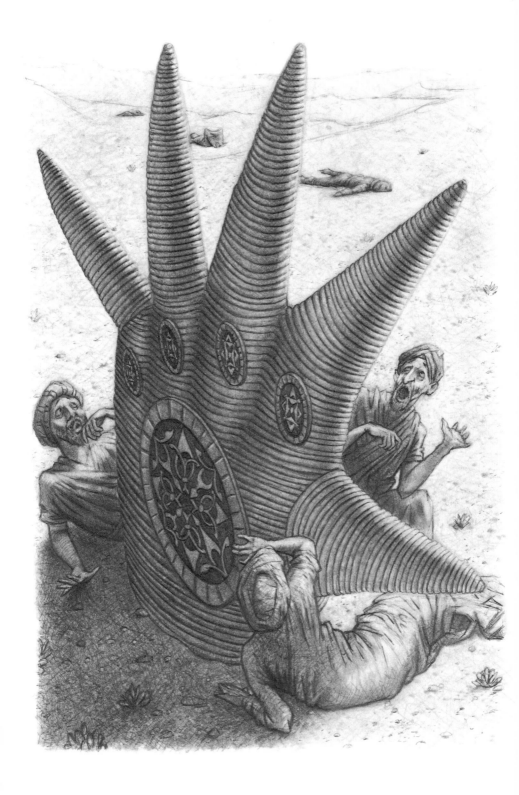

carefully. Maybe that hand might come alive, maybe make a grab at us. We stood there out of reach, staring at it. It was a wonderful thing, perfectly made, a blazing brass hand under the sun. All right, so one of us was going to have to go up and touch it. So—all ready to jump back at the slightest movement, one of us went up and *did* touch that giant brass hand, and then we all fell down flat in the sand—because it came alive and started to move. It was just sticking out by the wrist. The fingers didn't move, but the whole hand turned in the sand, wheeled around almost halfway in a circle, like there was someone deep under the sand with just his hand sticking out, a giant brass man, and he came awake with the touch, and turned slowly in some sort of enchanted fit, maybe thinking his time had come to be set free. Sort of pathetic when you think about it. But anyway, that hand turned and stopped. It seemed safe enough then, so we stood up and studied it. What did it mean?

"It came to us that the thumb was *pointing*, sticking out straight like that. It was pointing toward a high sand dune close by, and we ran off and climbed it. Just over the other side was a small pool of water, and we fell down and drank. Then one of my friends jumped up, gasped, doubled over clutching at his stomach, and fell down dead."

"Just you and one friend left alive," I said.

"Almost over," said Old Ali, nodding. "And same as before, we got no more than a swallow and that little pool sunk in the sand. And we walked away. Before long we were stretched out in the sun again, all dried up, and the voice came again, just like we expected, and this time it said, "See." We lifted our heads, eyes all crusted over and dry, squinting, and tried to see what there was to see. And not far away from us was a beautiful and strange thing. It was like the top of a crystal ball sticking out of the sand, like the top of a great bubble lifting up. We went over and kneeled down beside it. It was ten feet across or so. So clear, and so beautiful. We looked into it. It was brilliant and deep. Everything down in there was so far away, like you could almost see to the middle of the earth. And we looked, and we saw way down in there—a desert, and on that desert we could see two men kneeling on the ground, looking into the top of a large crystal ball, and it was us. It was us, like a picture of ourselves seen from up in the sky. There we were, down in the crystal depths of the thing, kneeling and looking. And as we looked, that picture became smaller and smaller, like it was going away, like we were getting higher and higher in the sky, until finally we were just little specks on the desert, down there in that crystal ball.

"But that was good, because having this view from way above ourselves, we could see a lot of the desert, and we saw that there was an oasis off a ways, and we could see which way it was from us.

"Well, we found that oasis. There were some trees, and some grass there, and a beautiful clear pool, large enough to bathe in. We stood at the edge of the pool for a moment, me and my last friend, looking at each other. It was a sort of good-bye, because we knew that one of us was going to die. Then we put our faces down to the water. It was peaceful the way my last friend died, and I was glad for that. He just rolled over in the cool grass, very gentle like, without making a sound, and he was dead. And I was alone."

The Silver Thread

"After drinking enough, I looked around. There was something about this place, this little oasis. It seemed to be a real place—not just some magic invention. The water in the pool didn't dry up, but stayed, and the trees were fresh, palm leaves moving in the little wind. And it seemed to me that I'd been there before. Seemed to me like I just might have an idea where I was, and how to get home. I stood up, walked around, trying to get a feel of where I was. Then, after drinking some more, I walked away from there, thinking I could always come back. It seemed the sort of place that would stay put, that you could depend on.

"But after I'd walked awhile, a wind came up and covered my tracks, and I knew I was lost again. I got dry so quick that I began to think that everything was all a dream, and not any of the water had been real. I began to think that we had never even heard that voice, or found any water at all, not any of all those times, and that my friends had all died in an ordinary way and nothing unusual, and that it was the hot sun doing things to my brains, steaming up all that strangeness, crystal balls, brass hands, sand that turned to water, and so forth. So I laid down, ready to die. If the voice came again, there was no one left to die except me, and I was too gone to care about it.

"When it did come, that voice, it sounded different. It was closer now, and like a real voice, not that great hollow sound out of nowhere and everywhere. I pushed myself up and sat looking. And there he was! He was like a ghost or something, with a white cloak pulled down to his toes and a hood pulled over his head, all dark and shadow inside, with no face I could see. I stood up, not saying anything. And this ghost, or man, put a hand inside his cloak and came out with a long silver needle, and looped in the needle was a long silver thread. He walked up to me and stopped.

"—Open your mouth, he said. I did, thinking he had some other strange way to give me water. But that wasn't it. Quickly he shot out a hand, stuck his fingers into my mouth and grabbed my tongue and yanked it out like it was a fish, and quick as that he stabbed that long silver needle through my tongue, and pulled the silver thread all the way up to the end, where there was a big knot in it. I yelled out and fell down on my knees because of the pain, and put my hands to my mouth.

"—Let it be, the man ordered me. —I will lead you out of the desert on this silver thread.

"I dropped my hands, blood on them, and he said these words:

"—The pain is to remind you that you must never

[82]

tell how your friends died out here in the desert, and how you were saved. For on the day you tell that story, you will die.

"That's all he said. Then he pulled on the silver thread, taking up the slack and jerking me to my feet, and started walking away, leading me like a goat. I was almost blind from the pain. We walked until it was dark, and sometimes I could hardly walk at all, sometimes just crawling, and getting up, and falling down again. And when I couldn't move anymore he'd give that silver thread a yank and I'd scream out loud, my tongue all swollen up with blood like a sponge, the front of me sprayed with my blood. But the pain always got me up. Then he'd say that thing again.

"—The pain is to remind you that you must never tell how your friends died out here in the desert, and how you were saved. For on the day you tell that story, you will die.

"I heard that warning several times, ears pounding, eyes nearly blind, stumbling like a man with broken legs, and we kept walking into twilight, and then into the dark. At last I smelled smoke, and out of my dim eyes I could see a lamp lit inside a tent not far off. We stopped. The man in the white robe let the silver thread go slack and walked up to me. He took hold of the thread next to my tongue, and yanked the knot right through. I fainted and fell down. How long I was fainted I don't know. I woke up choking on blood. My tongue was like a torn rag, and the man was gone. Coughing and gurgling, I crawled toward the tent. It had a large white star sewn on it. A young man and his wife were out in the desert on a pilgrimage, and they took me in and cared for me. For days afterward I couldn't talk, so of course I didn't tell them anything about what happened out there in the desert. And then at last I got home, and that's the end, and the Three Brothers lay where they lay, and for all I know are still out there lost in the desert."

"And you never searched for them again?" I asked.

"Devil take those cursed Horns!" Old Ali said. "I had some sense left. Let the fools chase 'em."

All Lies Maybe. Maybe Not.

Then he pressed his back into the boards, stretched his legs out, lifting them off the ground, and stretched all over, thumped his feet back down, crossed his legs, and looked out the door. The train was slowing down. Old Ali moved back from the door a little distance. I was thinking. There was something about that story . . . something I was trying to think of. . . .

"This is Pasco," Old Ali said as we rumbled across a steel bridge. "You might find some work here, but I'd go on up to Yakima."

And then I thought of it.

"Wait a minute," I said. "That story, that man who led you out of the desert. He said you couldn't tell what happened out there or you'd die that day you did tell. Then you should be dead, because you just told me."

Old Ali looked at me straight and steady and said, "That's right. But I've told that story before."

"Then why aren't you dead?"

"Because that's not how it happened," he said. "If I told you that, I believe I might just die. Can't be too careful, you know. I may be old but this train's going *somewhere*."

"Oh, no," I said. "All just a lie!"

I kicked my heels at the floorboards. I was disgusted with myself for being so taken in. Another good laugh for the old bum, Tex or Bob or whatever. I looked up with an angry look, expecting the old bum to be grinning at me, or chuckling at me. But he looked perfectly serious, even concerned.

"No, not a lie," he said. "I was out in the desert, like I said, and lost with five friends who died out there. But I can't tell you the true story of how that was, or how I got out. See—I can't take that chance telling it. I never did pray as much as I should have."

"And everything else was a lie, too," I cried, feeling betrayed. "The goats, the robber, the woman, the trumpets and everything . . . just lies."

"Here," he said. "Here—to believe." He rustled around in his old bummy pack then, and took out a little wooden box. The top was inlaid with ivory. Taking off the top, he reached down into it. He held up a small object. The train was coming to a stop in the yards.

"See," said Old Ali. He held up a small polished seashell. "Remember this? God does not forget his creatures."

Then he took a little dried blue flower out of the

box and held it up. "Remember this?" he said. "The eye of God is everywhere."

He put it back, reached in the box one more time, and brought out a small piece of amber, and inside it was a shimmering, iridescent purple beetle.

"Remember this," he said, "and think on your deeds."

The End of Summer

Just then a banging came on the side of our boxcar. I couldn't get up quick enough to hide, and a yardman with a two-foot stick was looking in at me.

"Okay, kid, haul out and hit the road," he said.

I scuttled over the open space, dragging my backpack, and I dropped out the door. The yardman put a hand on my pack, lifted it out, and poked me with his stick.

"Scram," he said. "Move your butt out of here."

"My pack," I said, putting a hand toward it.

"I got that," he said, pointing the stick into my face and glaring at me. Then he made a move like he was going to club me, and I ducked and ran off. I turned to look at him as he walked down the line of cars with my backpack hanging in his hand, laughing and laughing. I guess he missed seeing Old Ali in the boxcar.

I got out of the yards, walked off, and found a star route going north up toward Yakima, and hitched a ride with an old couple.

Well, I picked fruit in Yakima, cleared brush in Wenatchee, drove a truck in the Umatilla cornfields, spent a night in jail in Grand Coulee, ran scared out of Spokane, and in Moses Lake I fell in love.

Later that summer, traveling in Washington state, I came off Toppenish Ridge, across the Horse Heaven Hills, through a beautiful canyon, over Satus Pass to Goldendale, following along the Klickitat River to Lyle on the Columbia River, and along the Columbia to White Salmon, and across the Bridge of the Gods into Oregon.